I0732370

The Singularity series:

Redshift
The Observer Effect
Uncertainty Principle
Quantum Entanglement
Event Horizon
Point Singularity

Prequel
Ani, or, the care and feeding of your great tree-dwelling venomous tentacled land-devil

ANI

R.M. OLSON

ISBN-13: 978-1-990142-23-9

To Skullhead, Midnight, Nona Grey, and Riverdog.
Who are all ridiculous, but we love them anyways.

1

Aran shaded his eyes against the whipping snow, squinting vainly into the howling blizzard. "What did you say?" he shouted, tapping his wrist to activate the wavelink.

Istvay's reply through his earpiece was muffled and almost inaudible, but there was a distinct note of panic to it.

Probably 'something something something they were both about to die.' Which, in fairness …

Aran glanced behind him. Which was a mistake.

The ledge of snow towered above him, tall enough to almost tilt the sky, and he squeezed his eyes shut against the sudden wave of dizzying nausea, clinging to his ice pick with both hands.

Damn it.

Istvay was still shouting, the panic in their indistinct words growing more pronounced.

Why the hell had Aran thought this was a good idea?

With an effort, he opened his eyes and pried the fingers of one hand loose from his ice pick, reaching into the pocket of his heavy parka. He drew out the sensor and hit it against his thigh a few times, then turned the dial.

If he was right, though—

The sensor beeped, and he held it up to his face to peer at it through the blowing snow.

Then he grinned, the icy cold of the air making his teeth ache.

He squeezed his palm to activate his wavelink, and shouted, "Istvay! I think I found something!"

There was only crackling in return, which—well, probably made sense. Considering the conditions.

He glanced down to where his friend was anchoring him, almost invisible in the thick blizzard. Istvay was halfway up the mountain, but still several hundred metres below him. Their crampons, dug deep into the glacier ice on the steep slope, and their gloved fingers tight on the rope, were the only things keeping Aran from sliding to an untimely and expedited death if for one moment his hands slipped on his ice pick.

It would be a terrifying thought, normally. But he didn't really have the attention to think of it right now, because according to the sensor …

He tucked the sensor into his sleeve and, still dangling from one hand on the ice pick, brushed gently at the loose snow in the shallow horizontal crevasse the sensor had indicated.

A moment later, he saw it—the unmistakable purple flash.

Violet snow toads.

They were hibernating, and didn't even stir as he brushed back a little more of the snow, just enough to scan the sensor over top of them. Then he studied the readout, his heart pounding in excitement.

Violet snow toads were generally only found in the northern Rim Mountains. But some of the genetic tests he'd run on the populations up there suggested there was another subspecies.

And here they were.

His grin widened. The readout on the sensor had just confirmed it. Almost identical, but just enough variation.

A new subspecies.

He laughed in sheer delight, the icy wind catching the sound and whipping it from his lips as he stared down at the tiny, mottled purple backs of the toads, huddled together, each one barely the size of his thumbnail.

"You're beautiful," he whispered. Gently, he swiped a test-swab across the toads' backs, just enough contact to get some genetic material, and sealed it carefully for later testing. That, along with the visual documentation and the location, should be enough to get him started.

His brain was buzzing, the euphoria of his discovery filtering through his blood like alcohol.

"Pishti, we did it!" he shouted into his wavelink. Maybe they couldn't hear him, but if they could—

His wavelink crackled again, and he caught Istvay's frantic voice, although he still couldn't make out the words. He glanced down to see his friend waving their hands over their head, beckoning to him.

He looked up involuntarily at the massive sheet of snow towering over him, and then down to the long, almost sheer slope below.

He swallowed hard.

Damn it to hell.

As long as the only thing in his head was research, he could handle this. It was when he actually remembered where he was, and what he was doing in order to get the research—

For the briefest of moments, the crackling over the wavelink composed itself into words, Istvay's voice barely audible over the noise of the blizzard. "Aran! There's something wrong with the gear. You need to get down here, right now."

Aran took a deep breath, closing his eyes for just a moment.

He had everything he needed—enough genetic data, as well as all the scans. But now it was a matter of forcing himself back down the mountain.

He groaned, and muttered a halfhearted prayer.

This was always the hardest part.

Bracing himself, he grabbed his second ice pick from its strap on his snowsuit and drove it into the glacier half a metre below the first. His crampons scrabbled against the sheer ice for a moment before they caught, and gently, he lowered himself an arm's length down, then repeated the procedure, then again.

Istvay's voice through the wavelink was muted by the howling of the wind, but he caught something that sounded like, "For hell's sake, hurry up!"

He glanced down. And then he saw Istvay's face, turned up towards him, go slack with horror.

And at the same time, the rope holding most of his weight slipped.

With a resounding *crack* that sounded like a flare going off, the taut rope above him snapped, and Aran was skidding down the side of the glacier towards the sheer cliff at the bottom.

He swore breathlessly, jamming his ice picks into the side of the glacier to halt his slide. One of them caught, and just for moment he thought it would hold.

And then a falling chunk of snow slammed into him, knocking him sideways, and his hand was ripped loose from the pick.

For a few moments, there was nothing but the panicked, stomach-tightening sensation of falling, snow surrounding him, and no idea which way was up.

And then he hit the snow pack below him, the impact hard enough to knock the breath from his body, and he was rolling, head over heels, down the slope.

He'd lost both ice picks by now, and the frayed end of the rope was trailing behind him, wrapping around his body as he tumbled down the steep slope.

He was going to die. He was actually going to—

"Aran!" He heard Istvay's voice faintly through the blinding, whirling disorientation, and he caught the briefest glimpse of his friend stepping carefully out across the glacier towards him—

And then he slammed into something and came up short, the impact enough to knock the wind from him a second time.

For a moment he lay dazed, braced against something warm and soft, trying to figure out what the hell had happened.

And then he heard Istvay's strained grunt, and he blinked his eyes open to see his friend braced against the ice, one hand clinging desperately to an ice pick, legs spread for balance, their other arm wrapped around Aran, holding him steady.

"Aran. Are you alright?" Their voice was choked with effort.

"I'm—I'm fine—"

And then, from above, came a noise like nothing Aran had ever heard before; a heavy, tumbling roar that started low and then increased, until there was nothing in the world but the grinding wave of sound.

Aran looked up, and swore.

The entire mountain above him seemed to have come loose from its moorings, and was hurling itself in a rolling, heaving mass towards them.

Istvay shouted something that was probably profanity, but the noise of the avalanche was too great for Aran to make it out.

Damn. It must have been set off by the impact of his fall.

Aran's brain was spinning almost as fast as the snow above him.

He could feel Istvay turning, hunching their shoulders in a desperate, last-ditch effort to brace and save them both, somehow, but there was nothing to be done. They had about twenty seconds before the snow reached them, if that. And then they'd both be carried off the edge of the cliff along with the rest of the debris picked up by the roiling crest of the avalanche—

Aran's brain snapped back to a half-conscious memory, something he'd noticed without really taking note of it, too engrossed in the violet snow toads.

He struggled to his feet, wincing, and jammed his crampons into the ice, then grabbed Istvay's wrist, yanking them after him towards a dark hollow in the snow, barely visible through the swirling blizzard.

It had to be here. He had to have remembered right.

Istvay tossed him an ice pick, and he snatched it, jamming it into the ice and hauling himself up, then pulled Istvay up behind him. His friend's crampons slipped, and Istvay stumbled, Aran's grasp on their wrist the only thing holding them.

"Aran—" they gasped.

The snow was metres away now, the whirling crest of the avalanche almost like the tip of a wave, bubbling and foaming, carrying along with it the trees and rocks it had ripped loose in its careening trail of destruction.

With a final heave, Aran pulled himself over the lip of the depression.

He'd been right. It was a cave.

He yanked Istvay up behind him and shoved them into the dark opening, tumbling in after to land practically on top of them.

For a moment, everything was darkness and noise. It took Aran a moment to realize they were safe, the avalanche churning and foaming over the mouth of the cave, but leaving them protected inside the small air-pocket.

And then, finally, it was over.

Aran blinked, looking around him instinctively despite the pitchy blackness. After the horrific, ear-rending noise, the silence was almost jarring.

A dim light blinked on close beside his face, and Aran turned his head to see Istvay, the light glowing faintly from their palmscreen.

"Istvay," he said in a choked voice. "You're alive."

There was a long scrape across Istvay's cheekbone, and in the blue light of the palmscreen their face was wan and exhausted, but they managed a small smile.

"Looks like we both are, unlikely as that seems," they said.

Aran smiled back, reluctantly.

And then he glanced down, and realized he was still clutching Istvay's wrist, and Istvay was pushed up beside him, one arm flung around his waist as if to keep him from being carried away.

In the dim light of the palmscreen, Istvay's brown eyes under their long lashes looked darker than usual, and the shadows emphasized the sharpness of their cheekbones, the dark outline of the five o'clock shadow on their chin. Their full lips, only a few centimetres away from Aran's own …

His heart was pounding. He closed his eyes and forced his thoughts away.

"Are you alright?" Istvay sounded worried.

He opened his eyes to Istvay peering at him, pushed up on one elbow, their face concerned—

"I'm—I'm fine," he croaked, sitting up quickly and dropping his hand from Istvay's wrist as if it had burned him.

Istvay frowned, but didn't comment. And then they, too, seemed to realize how close they were, and they dropped their arm from around his waist and scooted back quickly.

There was an awkward silence, where neither of them seemed to want to look the other in the eye.

At last, though, Istvay cleared their throat. "We'd better get moving if we don't want to be trapped down here permanently," they said. "The snow is going to solidify pretty soon. I think our best bet is going to be to dig over there."

Aran fumbled in his supplies pouch and came up with the folding emergency shovel. "Sorry, it's the best I've got," he mumbled.

Istvay chuckled, a soft, warm sound that made Aran look away hurriedly. "I'm not much better. I think I have a cooking pot from lunch."

Aran grinned despite himself. "Well, I guess we'd better get to work, then. It's not going to get any easier."

By the time they'd extricated themselves from the cave, the round rim of the sun was nothing but an orange glow on the horizon. The stars were already faintly visible in the darkening blue-black of the sky, glowing off the stark white of the glacier and outlining the dark shapes of the tall peaks surrounding them.

Aran wiped the sweat from his forehead and glanced at Istvay surreptitiously. They didn't seem any more tired by the exertion than usual, and the small knot of worry in his chest loosened a little.

"Well," he said, "that's one way to keep warm."

Istvay laughed. "I'd rather just use one of the self-heating snowsuits, if it was an option."

Aran grinned at them, and glanced down at where their camp had been, once upon a time.

He sighed. "I suppose there's no reason to head back there now. And I guess so much for our brand new camp gear." He shook his head. "We've made an air hole now. May as well stay in the cave for the night, and figure out a way down tomorrow."

Istvay nodded, but there was a frown creasing between their eyebrows. "Speaking of equipment," they said. "Can I see the broken end of the anchor rope?"

Aran nodded, and passed it over.

Istvay studied it, their frown deepening. They held it out towards him. "Look at this. Do you see how the internal fibers are bunched together like that? This is the ravnor fibre. No wonder it failed—it's notorious for breaking in cold conditions."

Aran looked at them in surprise. "Ravnor?" He asked. "I thought —"

Istvay nodded grimly. "I asked specifically for the cold-weather gear. And they gave me the right stuff, I know, because I inspected it twice before I packed it for our trip. I must have missed it when I took it out this morning, because it was dark and the colours are almost identical."

Now Aran was frowning, too. "But this is the first time we used the ropes since we left Vila Nova do Sol. If you checked when you packed it—"

Istvay nodded again, their expression even grimmer than before. "It means," they said, "that someone tampered with our gear."

2

Aran leaned back against the cave wall, pushing his meagre dinner plate aside, and shook his head.

"Okay. Okay, I'm not trying to argue or anything. But—don't you think that's a bit unbelievable?"

Istvay dropped their head back against the wall of the cave. The flickering fire illuminated their features in a dancing glow, but even in the uncertain light Aran could see the expression, somewhere between fondness and absolute exasperation, that Istvay seemed to reserve specifically for him. "Aran. Listen to me. Between the time I bought the supplies and the time we left the city, the supplies never left my sight. Except one time. And that was when we were looking through some data at the university lab. Do you remember the only person who was in the lab with us?"

Aran frowned. "Emeric?" he hazarded. "But why would he ..."

Istvay blew out a long breath. "You do remember who we're talking about, right? Our old classmate? The one who hates you? The one who spent our entire university career hating you? The one who used to go to the professors and try to use his family's position to threaten them into lowering your grades, and who once paid off his friends to beat you up behind the student dorms, and who spread all those rumours about you, and who sabotaged your lab results three separate times? That Emeric?"

Aran was still frowning. "Okay," he said cautiously. "I know Emeric and I never exactly got along—"

"If by 'never got along,' you mean every time Emeric looked at you, he looked like he was having fantasies of intentional homicide," Istvay muttered.

Aran ignored them. "But we all graduated—what, four years ago? Surely he doesn't still care about all that. And even if he did, that doesn't mean that he would—" he broke off, shaking his head. "Why would he want to sabotage our equipment? I mean, surely it would be easier just to mess with our sensors or something. You didn't even notice the rope wasn't the same as the one you'd packed, so it's not like it would have stopped our expedition, it just would have …" he trailed off.

Istvay raised their head. "Exactly."

For a few moments, Aran was silent.

It was ridiculous. Yes, Emeric hated him—at least, he'd gathered that, although he'd never been entirely clear on the reasons. And Istvay certainly hated Emeric back, enough for both of them. But—

"But … killing me?" he said at last. "Doesn't that seem a bit—"

Istvay pinched the bridge of their nose, as if staving off a headache. "Aran," they said in that flat voice. "It's been—what, six months since you were called in front of the entire Council and given the system-wide Medal for Scientific Advancement? Emeric would have killed for something like that. Believe me. Did you see his face when the medal was being awarded? Because I did. If he thought he could get away with killing you—"

Aran shook his head stubbornly. "I just can't believe—"

Istvay threw up their hands in exasperation. "Aran! He is literally the only person who had access to our equipment. And, as you said, literally no other part of the expedition would have been sabotaged by him switching up the ropes, except for the fact that you would not have come back alive."

Aran was silent for a moment. "It—" he shook his head. "Look. I admit it looks suspicious. But it may have been just a coincidence. An accident or something."

"And the people who tried to jump us in the alley when we were going back to our hotel room after the awards?" asked Istvay. "Back to our hotel, which, by the way, Emeric had coincidentally gotten the address of only a couple hours earlier? And when our transport driver tried to rob us at knifepoint when we were in the city the time before last, and had an uncanny amount of knowledge about who we were and what our plans were?"

Aran sighed.

"Listen," said Istvay through their teeth. "I'm not trying to make you believe me. I'm just asking—I'm just asking you to think about it, okay?"

Aran hesitated, then, seeing the look on Istvay's face, nodded silently.

Istvay clearly believed Emeric wanted them both dead. And— well, as unlikely as it seemed, he couldn't necessarily refute any of Istvay's points.

Emeric hated him. That had been made abundantly clear. And Emeric was jealous of him, apparently, although why anyone would be jealous of the constant horde of reporters following him every time he tried to get into the city, the unavoidable notoriety that came with the award from the Council—honestly, if he could have given it up, he would have done it in a heartbeat. But apparently Emeric seemed to think it was something desirable.

Still, the thought of someone actually willing to kill him over it …

The rest of the evening was uncharacteristically quiet. Istvay was still scowling, and Aran wasn't entirely sure what to say either. But at least the cave itself was warm enough, small and packed in by snow as it was, and they had the two emergency blankets.

At last he and Istvay fell asleep back to back, the blankets draped over both of them.

Aran resolutely refused to think about the comforting, familiar warmth against his back in any other capacity than a way to keep both of them from freezing to death in the night.

He'd let himself think of more, once. And it had been a mistake, and he wasn't going to make it again, because he'd almost screwed everything up for good. And as much as his entire chest ached, sometimes, with longing—Istvay was his best friend. He wasn't going to lose them over something like that.

It took the two of them until halfway through the next day to get down to where their original camp had been at the base of the mountain—or at least, where they guessed it had been. The landscape had been altered so drastically by the avalanche that it was hard to know for sure.

"Well," said Istvay with a resigned sigh. "I guess we trek back to where we left the transport. It's only—" they glanced at their palmscreen. "Another nine hours of walking, give or take. And then I guess it's back to our base camp to resupply, since there's nothing left of what we brought other than what's in our supply pouches."

Aran glanced at his friend and cleared his throat. "Um. Listen, you're going to be … I mean, you're not …"

Istvay rolled their eyes. "Aran. I'm fine. I promise I'll tell you if I start feeling off, okay? We've talked about this, chances are I'll never get it."

"Yeah," Aran mumbled.

Istvay was right, the chance they had the genetic defect was low. He knew plenty of people whose parents had died from it, and who'd never developed even a symptom.

But if Istvay was going to start showing signs of it, it would be in the next year or so. And Aran would never get the sight out of his mind of Istvay's mother on her deathbed, the gauntness in her face, her body too weak for her even to roll over.

And he'd never get the worry out of his mind, that one day he'd wake up and Istvay's face would be a little more gaunt than it should be, and he wouldn't notice, and …

He shoved the thought from his mind. They'd both just survived an avalanche, dug out of an ice-cave, and trekked down a mountain, and Istvay didn't look any more tired than Aran felt.

When at last, soaked through and exhausted, the two of them were seated in the small transport, the warm air from the heater blowing against their numb fingers and toes and their clothes steaming from the moisture of the melting snow, the sun had long since set. The lights from the transport against the snow outside made the scene feel cozy and comfortable, and Aran leaned back, closing his eyes and letting the delicious heat turn his exhausted muscles to jelly.

"I transmitted our findings to the lab," he said, eyes still closed. "They should have them by now, and they'll be able to do a full analysis. I'm guessing they'll have some results for us by tomorrow night."

Istvay groaned. "I vote we sleep here tonight. I sure as hell don't want to try to make myself stay awake while I pilot the damn transport to our base camp." Their words were slurring with weariness.

"Agreed," mumbled Aran.

A small alert buzzed up his arm from the wavelink implanted in his wrist. He blinked his eyes open and frowned sleepily, squeezing his hand to activate his palmscreen.

Then he froze.

"Aran?" Istvay's voice seemed to come from a distance. "Is something wrong?"

Aran was still staring at his palmscreen. "Istvay," he whispered.

Istvay scooted closer to peer over his shoulder, face creased in concern.

Aran's heart was pounding so quickly he felt almost dizzy with it as he held up the screen to give them a better look.

"Istvay," he whispered again. "Look!"

Istvay glanced down at the screen, then back at Aran, frowning. "It's talking about land-devils. Which, thank every deity that exists, don't live on this planet."

"I know, I know. But look, Istvay! They say there's a hatching that's going to be taking place! Do you know how rare a land-devil hatching is? Every fifty or sixty years, I think they've hypothesized."

Istvay's frown deepened. "Aran! That isn't a scientific bulletin, it's a damn red-alert warning. It's from the transport bureau, to warn the spacecrafts to stay away from that side of the system for the next few weeks."

The excitement bubbling in Aran's stomach was as heady as champagne. "The hatching is supposed to happen in the next five days. A hatching, Istvay! No one has ever been able to observe a hatching!"

Istvay turned sharply to stare at him. "That's because if anyone had tried, they'd be dead. These are land-devils we're talking about!

Great tree-dwelling venomous tentacled land-devils. The things who have an entire planet to themselves, because we couldn't figure out a way to keep humans alive there for more than about ten minutes? Hell, they're the reason that entire side of the Joias system was never colonized. They're the most deadly creatures we as a species have encountered in the five damn centuries since we arrived in the system. You wouldn't survive getting onto their planet. If by some miracle you did, you'd have to trek through a thick forest inhabited mostly by land-devils and the creatures they hunt as prey. You'd be killed before you made it ten metres. And everyone who studies them hypothesizes they're highly protective of their nesting sites."

They looked at Aran more closely. "Aran. Listen to me. You can't seriously be considering—Aran, no! This is a terrible idea! There is a reason why no one has ever—"

"Pishti." Aran felt almost starry-eyed. "Pishti, imagine! I've never seen one of them before in real life. And to watch a hatching? Can you imagine the kind of data we'd get from that?"

"Who the hell sent this to you?" Istvay mumbled. They grabbed Aran's wrist, pulling it closer to inspect his palmscreen. Then they swore, dropping Aran's hand. "Aran." Their voice was flat. "Emeric sent it. That alert isn't supposed to go to anyone but the transportation minister. The lab back in do Sol would have just received your data from this expedition, which means Emeric just found out you survived his damn sabotage. And he immediately sends this to you. Don't you find that maybe just a little suspicious?"

Aran frowned, glancing down at the screen. "Maybe he meant to send it someone else. Or—or maybe he felt bad about the equipment. Maybe this was him apologizing."

"Aran! This is not Emeric apologizing! He knew exactly how you'd react to this. This is Emeric trying to kill you! Again!"

Aran was still staring at the notification on his palmscreen.

His whole life, ever since he'd first heard of them, he'd wanted to see one of the land-devils in the flesh. He'd never been able to, of course, because something about they were dangerous enough to wipe out the entire human population of Colorida or something ridiculous like that, and how do you ask permission from the government for something like that? As if an animal's value was based solely on its relationship to humans. But this, the hatching … this could possibly be his chance. They'd be able to gather massive amounts of data, expanding their knowledge of the creatures exponentially with this one expedition. Enough data that it might possibly induce even the Council to approve a request.

"If we sent a request in right away, we might get permission in time." His voice was almost trembling with excitement. "Can you imagine, Istvay?"

Istvay made a strangled sound.

Aran was already paging quickly through the information on his screen. "It's only a twenty-four-hour space-flight, if we can get a decent ship. We have five days. If they take too long it won't work, but if you talk to that one friend of yours in transport—"

"Aran! What part of this are you not understanding? We are not going to see the hatching! That is a terrible idea. Hell, the only reason we even know about it is that somebody who hates you, and, we have already established, wants you dead, sent you the information. I'm a hundred percent certain Emeric knew you'd have this exact reaction. He wants you dead, Aran! He almost bloody killed you less than twenty-four hours ago! And besides, it would mean you'd have to get on a ship and go out into space, which you hate."

"Pishti," Aran said pleadingly. "Pishti, we've never had a chance like this before. You know we'd never normally get permission. We'd be able to watch a land-devil hatching! Just think …"

Istvay groaned, covering their face with their hands.

Aran grinned and scooted closer, pulling Istvay's hands away from their face like he used to do when they were both kids, and he was trying to talk Istvay into something. "Pishti, please. Come on, this is an incredible opportunity."

"Stop calling me Pishti," they said through their teeth. "You know damn well I can't be mad at you when you do that."

Aran made his expression even more pleading, trying to hold back his grin. "Pishti. Pishti, Pishti, Pishti, Pishti, Pishti. Please, Pishti, just for me—"

Istvay yanked their hands back and shoved him away halfheartedly. "I hate you, Aran," they grumbled.

"No you don't. Come on, Pishti, I'm your best friend, I've wanted to do this my whole life, you can't say no to that, can you? You said you couldn't be mad when I called you Pishti."

Istvay closed their eyes and tipped back their head. "Dammit, Aran, you and your damn puppy-dog eyes. It's not fair of you to take advantage of me like this."

"So we can go?"

Istvay groaned again. "Why are you so damn adorable when you want something? I'm going to regret this, for the rest of my life, even though I doubt that'll be that long. We're both going to die horribly. You know that, right?"

Aran just grinned, too giddy with excitement to speak.

Istvay sighed. "Fine. Fine, Aran. I'll talk to my friend in transport and try to get us permission. But don't tell me I didn't warn you."

Aran whooped, grabbed Istvay's hands, and pulled them to their feet, dancing them around the cramped cabin. And despite Istvay's obvious attempts at a scowl, they were grinning too.

3

It took three days for the notice to arrive. Aran could hardly sleep for excitement the entire three days. Every morning, he checked his palmscreen to see if he had a message, and then found Istvay and checked their palmscreen.

"Do you know how much of a hassle it is to even try for this stupid permit?" Istvay grumbled. "Do you know how many hoops I've had to jump through just to get our names in front of the right people?"

"You're my best friend, Pishti," said Aran, grinning and bringing over a mug of steaming coffee. "Did I tell you that? The very best friend I've ever had in my entire life."

And then, finally, a notification came through.

Istvay stared down at their palmscreen for a few moments with an unreadable expression on their face.

Aran could hardly breathe.

At last Istvay sighed and stood. "Well," they said, and in the short pause Aran thought his heart might stop beating completely. "They approved it."

There was a tone in their voice that said that they didn't consider this cause for celebration.

Aran hardly cared. He was out of his seat in a moment, grabbing

Istvay by the wrist and dancing around the tiny kitchen of their rundown hotel room. "You're a damn genius, Istvay! I can't believe you got us permission!"

"I'm an idiot, you mean," Istvay grumbled, but they couldn't hide their own grin. "I can't believe they actually approved that. And, by the way, they sent a list about ten kilometres long of all the restrictions: we can't touch anything, we can't let the ship touch anything, we have to take a sanitizing shower and send in skin-swabs to be tested before we'll be allowed back in-atmosphere on Colorida —"

Aran nodded impatiently. "I know, I know. But Pishti!"

Istvay rolled their eyes heavenward. "It will be the most interesting scientific expedition we've ever been on, blah blah blah …" But they couldn't entirely disguise the excitement in their own voice.

"Alright," said Aran, letting go of Istvay's wrist and glancing around quickly. "We'll have to pack a few days' supplies and make sure we have enough equipment to gather data. And we'll have to find a ship to take us, which might not be as easy as it sounds, and then—"

Istvay sighed. "I've already taken care of it," they said ruefully. "I got everything ready, just in case the damn approval came through on time. There's a ship waiting for us down at the loading docks, and it's already packed up. And I made damn sure that Emeric doesn't know where it is."

Aran stared at them for a moment, completely speechless.

"Did I mention you're my very best friend?" he said at last, when he'd found his voice again. "I don't know if I mentioned that before. But Pishti, you're the very best friend in the world."

A few hours later, Aran stood in front of the small ship.

His heart was pounding again, but this time it was not from excitement.

He took a deep breath, closing his eyes.

It was alright. It would be fine. It was just space travel, just a short little jaunt. People took trips like this all the time. It was no problem at all, and there was no reason to worry …

None of this was convincing his nervous system. The adrenaline pounding through his body was enough to make him sick to his stomach, and there was a raw horror building in his chest that, if he couldn't hold it back, would completely overwhelm him, choking him, cutting off his breath, tightening his ribcage until his lungs had no room to expand.

He took a deep breath, and then another.

There was a hand on his shoulder, and he started, opening his eyes.

Istvay stood beside him, a fond, slightly rueful expression on their face. "Don't worry," they said quietly. "I'll be piloting, and you can go in the back and close the hatch and scream as loudly as you need to."

Istvay could, he knew, use this as an excuse to try to talk him out of this trip. Some small, terrified part of him wished they would.

But—

But, well, the thing was, Istvay was his best friend. They always had been, ever since the two of them were about five years old. And Istvay was still his best friend, even when he was being a complete and utter idiot, as, he was increasingly beginning to suspect, was the case right now. And they'd never do that to him.

He sucked in a shallow breath, taking strength from the warmth of their hand on his shoulder.

"Come on," Istvay said, and Aran nodded, forcing his legs to move him up the loading ramp of the small ship.

Thankfully, Istvay had managed to threaten, bribe, or sweet-talk the officials they'd gotten the permission from to keep the trip out of the news cycle. Which honestly was probably in the best interest of everyone involved—Aran didn't follow politics too closely, but thinking about it, he doubted anyone would want to be the politician who was responsible for letting someone fly out to view the land-devils in their natural habitat if things went sideways.

But at least that meant there were no reporters to see them off.

That was definitely a net positive, Aran thought to himself as he sat hunched into a ball in the back compartment of the ship.

He could hear, through the closed door in front of him, Istvay going through the ship's start-up sequence. Istvay had piloted before, and this ship was outfitted with a state-of-the-art autopilot. It wasn't that Aran doubted his friend's ability. It was just—

It was just—the fact of it. The cold, empty, horrifying void of space. The lifeless emptiness, the knowledge that out there all his expertise, all his knowledge, all his ingenuity could do nothing against the creeping blackness, the hollow vacuum that spread like entropy.

Damn it to hell. Why hadn't he considered this more? It wasn't like Istvay hadn't warned him. It wasn't like he hadn't known this was coming. He'd just been so excited …

There was a soft jolt as the engine started, then the stomach-dropping burst of acceleration as they shot upward through the planet's atmosphere. The ship shuddered, then calmed as they passed through the atmosphere and out into space, and Aran closed his eyes and clenched his teeth, squeezing his hands into fists, and tried to force himself to keep breathing.

It would be fine. It would be fine, Istvay knew what they were doing—

He could feel the icy tendrils of terror at the edge of his brain, its clutching fingers trying to pull itself out from his subconscious and take over in a screaming, blinding panic, where he couldn't think, or see, or feel, or—

"Aran." The voice seemed to come from far away. "Listen, Aran, I'm going to touch you. Is that okay? Nod your head if that's okay."

Aran managed a small, shaky nod, and then he felt Istvay's hands on his shoulders.

"Aran, we're going to breathe, okay? We're going to breathe together. Ready?"

Again, Aran managed a weak nod.

"Good." Istvay's voice was soothing. "Good. Now, with me, okay? In, two, three, four, five, six, seven.… Now out, two, three, four, five, six, seven. Good. Good, Aran, you're doing good. Again."

Finally, Aran managed to crack his eyes open, the pounding panic in his chest pushed back just a little.

Istvay was crouched in front of him, their hands on his shoulders, their eyes dark with concern. But when he caught their gaze, they smiled, and it was almost shocking, the relief that familiar smile brought.

"Better?" they asked, with their small, crooked grin.

Aran nodded without speaking.

Istvay squeezed his shoulder. "Good. It's going to be a short flight, don't worry. You stay back here, I'll let you know when we're back in-atmosphere to land. I'll need you up front with me then, because there are a few procedures I can't do on my own. Think you can handle that?"

Aran took a deep breath and managed his own shaky smile. "Yeah," he said. "Yeah, I think I can do that."

Istvay squeezed his shoulder again, then pushed themself to their feet. "Good. You have a few hours, I'll let you know when we're getting close. I'm going to get some sleep, and you should probably do the same, if you can."

They stepped through the door and back into the cockpit, and Aran stared after them, his entire body shaky with a mixture of residual adrenaline and sick relief.

By the time Istvay called him into the cockpit, he'd managed to get himself a little more under control. And it helped that, by the time he got there, they were already through the atmosphere.

At least, it probably helped. He hated heights, too, but not with the visceral terror he had of space. And besides—as he looked down on the thick green canopy that covered the planet where the land-devils lived, the bubbling excitement that had been lying dormant under the sick terror of spaceflight was beginning to reassert itself.

"We're going to put down right here," said Istvay, tapping the map on the control panel. "Apparently, they can sense heat, and noise disturbs them. But we can't land too far away, because statistically, we're not going to survive more than about a kilometre of walking on this damn planet. So we'll have to turn the engine off and coast the last kilometre or so, and then, as soon as we're on the ground, we'll hit the exterior coolant system on full. That should cool the ship enough so that they're not attracted to it. Then we'll need to wait inside the craft for about half an hour and watch the sensors to make sure that they haven't come over to check us out. And then we can put on the hazmat suits and go find the nest. We have the coordinate readings from the lab that monitors the planet and sends out the warnings."

Aran nodded, only half-listening. He was going over in his head the data he'd read on the land-devils, everything scientists had learned about them over the last five centuries.

It wasn't much. But it was utterly fascinating, nonetheless.

The excitement lasted through the landing sequence, and the half-hour wait to be sure they wouldn't be immediately killed upon stepping out. And then, at last, he and Istvay looked at each other, and Istvay gave him a wry nod.

He hit the controls, and the ship's hatch hissed open.

The air that wafted inside was wet and fetid and smelled of decaying vegetation.

It made sense. All the information they had indicated the nesting site was on the outskirts of the planet's largest swamp. He hypothesized a need for a high level of air humidity for the eggs, but it could also simply be that the swamp provided a plentiful supply of food.

"You have the equipment?" Istvay whispered.

Aran nodded. The excitement was almost enough to choke him.

"Alright," said Istvay with a sigh. "We may as well get going."

Istvay stepped off the loading ramp, sinking ankle-deep into the muddy swamp water. Aran jumped out after them, grabbed their arm, and dragged them bodily onto a patch of relatively dry ground just as a pair of jaws snapped on the empty air where Istvay had been standing a moment before.

Istvay swore under their breath. "I already hate this place," they grumbled.

Aran was grinning too broadly to speak.

The two of them managed to get onto drier ground without further incident and made their careful way through the thick trees and choking undergrowth towards the spot where their information indicated the nesting grounds were located. Aran's bush-knife was out, and every few steps he had to cut through another thick vine or overhanging branch just to make a passage wide enough for the two of them to wriggle through.

Insects swarmed around them, droning incessantly, and sweat trickled down the inside of his suit and helmet. Behind him, Istvay cursed quietly as they picked their way through the dense trees.

"No, Aran. I'm not dying. I just bloody hate this place," they snapped at him when he glanced back at them in concern.

The distance was just under a kilometre. But it took three hours of bone-breaking labour, and Aran's hands were raw with blisters by the time they reached the small clearing in the swamp.

He pushed through the curtain of hanging vines, and stopped, completely frozen in awe.

A massive web-nest had been strung in a copse of trees in the centre of the clearing. Through the gauzy webbing, they could see the small, wrinkly shape of what must be the eggs.

Aran dropped to the ground behind a massive fallen log, his hands trembling with excitement as he set up his sensors. Then he pulled the binoculars out of his equipment pouch and held them up to his eyes, dialling them in.

Sure enough, the shapes he saw were eggs. He counted six of them, and he could see, through the wrinkled, partially translucent reptilian shells, hints of movement, shadows of tiny tentacles wriggling over each other.

Istvay had dropped down beside him and taken out their field notepad.

Somehow, Aran managed to tear his eyes away from the nest. He handed Istvay the binoculars, then squeezed his hand to activate his palmscreen so he could jot down notes as well.

It didn't appear that the adult land-devils were present at the moment. As far as they knew, land-devils, male and female both, watched their nests closely, but the scent-markers he and Istvay had prepared for their suits should hide their scent relatively well if they didn't get too close. As long as they were completely quiet, the land-devils shouldn't know they were there.

He frowned, checking one of the sensors.

There were heat signatures, though—

Then a grin split his face, and he nudged Istvay. "It's the webs," he whispered. "The nest is radiating its own heat. That's how they must keep the eggs warm when they leave to get food." He retrieved his binoculars, and focused them to one side of the nest, where a collection of—well, it wasn't entirely apparent at first glance what they were. When he looked closer, though, it was clear they'd once been animals of some sort.

He'd read, of course, of how land-devils fed—injecting their prey with digestive juices strong enough to melt bone, and then sucking out the resultant slurry. But he hadn't heard of the digestive juices actually preserving the food.

Still, some of those creatures had clearly been there for more than a day or two, and he could catch no telltale whiff of decay.

"Do you think the hatchlings prefer decayed food, or do you think the digestive juices act as preservatives?" he whispered to Istvay, pointing.

Istvay frowned. For all their protests of earlier, they were clearly finding this fascinating as well. "I'm not sure," they whispered back. "I don't smell anything rotting, though. I'll watch the sensor, see if I pick up methane gas—"

Aran nodded, turning back to his observations.

When he blinked up again, the sun had very nearly set.

It had felt like no more than five minutes, but they must have been here for hours.

He moved gingerly, and at the sudden stinging cramp in his leg, he realized that it had, indeed, been hours.

Through the trees, he could hear the quiet chirp and hum of creatures preparing for the night.

And then, in the glow of the setting sun, he noticed something lying half-buried in the swamp water beneath the nest.

He fixed his binoculars on it, frowning. Then he poked Istvay in the ribs. "Istvay! Look. It must've fallen out of the nest."

Istvay glanced over.

The egg had fallen into a tangle of tree roots, and it lay half-submerged in the murky swamp water.

Death was a part of nature—Aran knew that as well as anyone, and better than some. But still, the sight of the tiny, helpless egg sparked a melancholy in his chest.

A pair of land-devils would only nest once in their lifetime, and for this egg to be lost, so close to hatching …

He glanced at it again, dialling up the magnification of the binoculars.

Then he hissed in a quick breath. "Istvay! It's still alive, look!"

Istvay took the binoculars and frowned, studying the egg. "For now," they said quietly. "It won't hatch out, not if what we know is correct. The eggs won't hatch unless they're warm."

Aran took back the binoculars, still watching the egg intently. "Maybe the parents will get back in time—" he began.

As if on cue, the forest around them grew silent. Aran looked up in time to see a graceful shadow ghosting through the trees above them, and then it dropped down into the nest.

Aran could hardly breathe.

She was beautiful.

The female land-devil's skin had taken on the colour and texture of her surroundings, without even the trace of orange surrounding the eye-pouches that marked the males of her species. Her bulbous body was the grey-green of the leaves and the mottled, pebbly surface of the tree bark, but as she settled into the nest, her skin turned gradually to a smooth, deep green. Her tentacles, long and delicate, with slender tips as graceful as a musician's fingers, stroked the eggs gently as she peered at her offspring with her protuberant eyes.

Aran's heart was pounding hard enough he thought maybe the vibration would give them away, and he was smiling so wide the muscles in his cheeks ached.

He'd never thought he'd see one. He'd never in his life imagined he'd see this beautiful, graceful, astounding creature.

She peered around again, as if checking that her nest was safe, then she swarmed down the tree to the spot where he'd seen the abandoned egg.

Even from here, Aran could see the tiny hatchling wriggling inside the semi-translucent shell, its movements slow and weak.

The female made a sort of growling purr, a pleading, sorrowful sound, and Aran's heart ached. She stroked the egg with the tips of her tentacles, and he waited for her to pick it up …

But she didn't.

With a last sorrowful growl, she pushed it deeper into the cold of the swamp, as if trying to hide it from her own view, then swarmed back up the tree to her nest.

"Istvay," he said, his voice choking, just a little. "Do you think—"

Istvay shook their head grimly. "I know you read the same things I did, Aran. They don't take back their eggs once they fall out of the nest. If an egg falls, it's guaranteed to die. And if it's the reason scientists hypothesize—risk of bacterial contamination for the other hatchlings—if we were to touch it, it would only contaminate it worse. Look at her. If she was going to take it back, you know she would have already."

"But if we could just get it somewhere warm so it could hatch on its own—"

Even as he said it, he knew it was hopeless. But he couldn't help himself. The tiny hatchling inside the translucent shell looked so helpless, and the mother land-devil so sad—

"They need to be fed by their parents for the first six or eight months of life," said Istvay. Their voice was patient, even though they must know Aran already knew the answer. "I'm sorry. I hate it too, but there's nothing we can do to help."

The male land-devil joined the female a few minutes later, and they caressed each other with the tips of their tentacles, making soft chirruping sounds as they watched their remaining eggs.

And then one of the tiny eggs began to wriggle, and Aran gave a small, inaudible gasp, his chest tight with a mixture of excitement and pure joy.

The egg wriggled more violently, and then something that must have been an egg tooth ripped a small, jagged hole in the shell. A moment later, the tip of a tiny tentacle poked through.

There were tears welling in Aran's eyes, for some reason, and he had to blink them away.

The two adult land-devils were purring and crooning at the emerging hatchling. The infant gave a tiny chirrup, and Aran's heart fluttered at the sound. With infinite tenderness, the father helped his infant peel away the shell while it chirped back at him in tiny baby tones that made Aran almost choke.

Another hatched, and then another, until there were six baby land-devils. The parents were crooning to them, gathering them close with their tentacles, the picture of a loving family.

All except for the tiny egg that had been lost. The one destined never to hatch, because in the swamp water, it would never have that opportunity. The hatchling that would die in the shell.

He pulled his eyes away from the sad scene and back up to the family group in the nest.

The parents stroked and preened and crooned, and Aran felt something soft and happy rising in his chest, despite the sharp pang of regret.

Carefully, the mother detached one of the stored dissolved prey, lowering it into the nest, and immediately the infants scuttled over, piercing the unfortunate creature's skin with their tiny beaks and squealing and chirping as the half-digested substance gushed out in a messy, and admittedly bloody, feast.

The adults watched for a few moments, but when the second creature had also been devoured, the female land-devil lifted herself up on the tips of her tentacles and swarmed up to the top of a tree. She launched herself from the tree branch and glided, catching the branch of the next tree and swinging herself gracefully along.

Aran watched her in absolute awe.

The male settled down into the nest, but after several minutes, he perked up, his protuberant eyes peering around suspiciously. After a few moments, he pulled himself out of the nest and disappeared silently into the trees, his motions as graceful and powerful as those of the female.

Again, the forest was silent, but eventually, the chirps and hums and buzzes of the smaller creatures began to reassert themselves.

And then, in the swamp water by the abandoned egg, Aran could see the reptilian eyes and elongated snout of the water-dwelling creature that had almost eaten Istvay when they landed.

No one had studied the creatures on this planet in any depth—the first colony of humans who tried to put down here to terraform had been entirely wiped out within twenty-four hours, as had the second, and when the third had made it out with only a couple of survivors, no one had seemed interested enough in the unique flora and fauna to come back.

But this thing was obviously some sort of water-dwelling predator. The presence of the adult land-devils had kept it away, but now that they were gone, momentarily—

The creature was approaching the egg, its beady eyes small and slitted.

The tiny hatchling inside the egg had obviously sensed some danger, because its weak wriggling had turned into a frantic thrashing.

"Pishti," Aran whispered.

A glance at Istvay's face told him they didn't like watching this any more than he did, but they shook their head grimly.

The reptile opened its mouth.

The tiny creature inside the egg gave a last, desperate wriggle—

And Aran, without having really consciously decided to do so, jumped to his feet and took the three splashing steps towards the tiny egg, his bush-knife already out and opened. He slashed through the tangle of roots, twisting his knife to get a better angle, slashed again, and then a third time. The roots popped free, and he snatched the egg up in his gloved hands, yanking his arm out of the way just as the predator's teeth snapped closed.

Istvay was on their feet, glaring at him and shout-whispering, "Aran, what the hell—"

But nestled in Aran's gloved palm lay the small, wrinkled egg. Safe.

The tiny hatchling inside stirred weakly, and Aran's entire heart melted.

Istvay was shouting now, having given up any pretence of keeping quiet.

It was only then—only when Istvay's voice penetrated the thick, rosy haze that seemed to suffuse Aran's vision as he watched the tiny creature, whose movements had grown slightly stronger now that it was in his warm hand—that he realized that the forest around them had once again gone silent.

Istvay was splashing through the swamp towards him, heedless of whatever might live in the waters. They grabbed Aran's shoulder and jerked him around, shouting something at the top of their voice.

Aran looked up, into the face of a very, very angry mother land-devil.

And he was standing right under her nest.

4

Istvay yanked Aran backwards as the land-devil hissed, eye pouches puffing out. Acid sprayed down on the place where he'd been standing, making the swamp water boil around his feet.

"Go!" Istvay shouted in his ear, and then the two of them were running. Aran paused for just long enough to scoop up the sensors as they passed, and then he was following Istvay, stumbling and tripping over fallen logs and vegetation.

They headed for the ship, following the trail they'd cut earlier, the land-devil hard on their heels. She swung from tree to tree, the skin-flaps between her tentacles spread as she leapt and glided after them. Her teakettle hissing echoed through the jungle—the only sound, besides the frantic rustle of animals making themselves scarce.

Aran risked a glance over his shoulder as she reared up, her body an angry lime-green streaked with red. He grabbed Istvay by the sleeve, yanking them behind a tree as she spat. The tree melted, the acid cutting through the bark like a knife.

Then he and Istvay were running again.

"How—the hell—does she move—so fast?" gasped Istvay.

"I don't know," Aran panted. "But I have my sensor going, and I'm hoping it'll pick up enough readings that—"

"It was a rhetorical question!" Istvay growled, managing to sound irritated even out of breath as they were.

Istvay leapt over a fallen log, and Aran, his bush-knife already out, sliced through a tangle of vines ahead of them, ducking through and pulling Istvay after.

"Keep moving!" he shouted. "She's not going to give up now she has our scent."

Istvay nodded, too breathless to speak.

The shadow of the land-devil passed over them like the shadow of a bird.

Aran grabbed the back of Istvay's jacket, forcing both of them to a skidding halt, and before they had time to react, he grabbed a glove from his supplies pouch and heaved it as far into the woods as he could. He and Istvay stayed frozen for just a moment, hardly daring to breathe.

Then there was the rustle of branches as the land-devil went after the decoy.

Istvay grabbed Aran by the shoulder, and they ran again.

Aran's legs were stumbling with wariness, his lungs burning, his chest aching like someone had jabbed a spike through it. There was a cramp in his side that flicked raw pain through his ribcage every time he sucked in a breath, but he didn't have time to worry about it, because damn it to hell, they were both about to die.

He couldn't resist a quick glance over his shoulder, though, watching as the land-devil, who'd apparently discovered their trick, leapt after them with graceful bounds that ate the distance effortlessly.

"She's gorgeous," he gasped, and Istvay turned to scowl at him.

"Your data isn't going to be any use to science if we die here. Because no one's damn well coming after us," they snapped.

Aran nodded and kept running.

The land-devil was covering the distance between them far too quickly. But they only had a few hundred metres left to go. He could see the ship in the distance, even through the tangle of trees. They were almost there …

And then she was above them again, and Istvay yanked him to the ground. He landed in the mud, Istvay on top of him, as the land-devil dropped to the ground in front of them, hissing and bridling. The pouches under her eyes were bulging, and she was clearly furious—clearly the only reason they were still alive was that she couldn't seem to decide who to kill first.

She lunged. Aran shoved Istvay out of the way and scrambled backwards, yanking up a branch to fend her off. It would only last for a moment, but if she was after him, it meant she wasn't going after Istvay, and maybe his friend would still have a chance to make the ship …

And then something large and soft was flung over the land-devil. She gave an undignified squawk, and he recognized the thing as the jacket from Istvay's protective suit. Then Istvay had him by the wrist and was hauling him to his feet, and the two of them were running once again.

They reached the craft and stumbled up the loading ramp, the land-devil scant metres behind, and the hatch slamming shut almost caught the tips of her tentacles.

Istvay gasped in relief and staggered into the cockpit, Aran close behind.

And then they both jumped in surprise as the land-devil landed heavily on the cockpit window, her tentacles suckering down against the plex.

"What the hell—" Istvay began, and then her sharp beak

hammered into the thick plex. "Aran," they said grimly. "She's not going to be able to—"

Aran was bent over, trying to regain enough air to speak. He was halfway-dizzy from the run, his heart thundering in his chest, his legs so weary he could hardly move them, but he managed to shake his head. "I—I don't know," he gasped. "But it's technically possible she could—"

Her beak hammered down again.

Istvay swore. "Well, either way, we sure as hell aren't going to make it off the planet like this. She's suckered down on the oxygen intake. I can't get it running until she's off."

"Give me—give me just a sec," Aran panted. He staggered to the emergency cabinet, yanked out a handful of flares, scanned them, and grabbed the two most likely looking. "I need you to open the hatch again."

Istvay nodded. "Make it quick, then. Because she's damn fast, if you hadn't noticed."

Aran stumbled to the hatch as it creaked open. He smacked the end of both flares to ignite them and tossed them in the direction of the land-devil.

Alone, he wasn't sure either of them would have worked. But the combination of a thunderous clap of sound and the burst of light brilliant enough to leave starbursts on the back of his eyelids startled the creature enough that, for just a second, she let go.

Istvay hit the ignition, and seconds later, the ship was blasting upwards towards the limit of the atmosphere.

When they were out of atmosphere and back in space at last, Istvay slumped over the controls. "I can't believe we actually did that," they groaned. "I can't believe we actually just—"

They paused, peering down at Aran's hands. "Your gloves," they said, frowning. "They're smoking."

Aran glanced down, then yelped and stripped off the gloves, tossing them onto the floor. His hands were thankfully unburnt, but the gloves had been melted almost through.

Istvay stared down at the melted gloves, a look of horrified realization dawning on their face. "Aran," they said slowly. "Please. Please tell me that you dropped the egg back in the swamp—"

Aran couldn't quite meet their eyes. "Pishti," he began.

He could already tell this conversation was not going to go well.

Istvay just stared at him, their expression completely blank.

He sighed. "Pishti, listen. The parents wouldn't have taken it back, not once it had fallen out of the nest, remember? And that thing in the swamp was about to—"

"You brought the egg back." Istvay's voice was as flat as their expression.

Aran shifted uneasily. "It's just a baby. I couldn't exactly—"

"You brought it back. We were being chased through the forest by a mother land-devil, who was trying very hard to kill us, and that whole time you were holding onto an egg that will hatch out a creature just like the one trying to kill us, and you brought it back. To our ship."

"What? Did you want me to just leave it to die?" Aran asked in some irritation.

Istvay was still staring at him. "Yes. Yes, that's exactly what you should have done. You should have left it to die, Aran, because those things are the most dangerous creatures in our entire solar system! In fact, as far as we know, they're the most dangerous creatures in ANY solar system. Our ancestors almost moved on from this entire galaxy, after having set up a colony, built cities, and terraformed multiple planets, because they were so damn terrified of these things, and rightly so! What the actual hell were you thinking?"

Aran sighed and slumped back in his seat.

It wasn't that Istvay was wrong, exactly. But—

"I couldn't just leave a baby to starve to death," he said pleadingly. "Besides, it's not like we don't have somewhere to keep it. We can just go straight back to our base camp, as soon as they give us clearance to land. That kennel we used for the sea-spines—that should hold up even to land-devil acid. They're very intelligent, I'm sure we'll be able to train this one so it isn't a threat …"

Istvay had closed their eyes and dropped their head back against the pilot seat, and they were pressing their thumb and forefinger against their temples, as if staving off a headache. "This was exactly the kind of thing the permit was meant to prevent," they said. "This is exactly why they don't give permission for people to go to that planet, ever. If we get back, and they find that, despite our clean skin-swabs and sanitizing shower, you have a baby land-devil tucked in the cargo compartment of the ship—a baby land-devil, I might remind you, inside an egg coated with an acid powerful enough that it's probably, at this moment, as we speak, trying to eat its way through the shell of our damn craft—" they groaned. "We are breaking so many laws, Aran. We're probably breaking every law that's ever been made in this entire system. When we get back, we are going to be the most wanted people on Colorida, and for good reason. We're going to get our butts thrown in jail so fast we won't even have time to—"

From the cargo hold behind them, there was a faint, sweet chirrup.

Istvay and Aran stared at each other. Then, slowly, Istvay got to their feet and stepped over to the cargo door. They pulled it open, Aran hovering behind them, and the two peered cautiously inside.

The egg was so translucent now they could see every feature of the tiny hatchling squirming and wriggling inside. One of its bulging eyes was open, and it was peering at them through the shell with a look that held so much pleading that Aran's entire heart turned to putty.

He turned to Istvay.

He thought he might be actually crying.

"Pishti," he whispered. "Look at it. It's beautiful. It's … isn't it the most amazing thing you've ever seen in your life? Something like that —that's worth going to jail for."

Istvay wasn't looking at the egg. Instead, they were studying Aran, and there was an expression on their face that was part fondness, and part sadness, and part something that Aran couldn't figure out, and wasn't sure he wanted to.

"Yes," they said quietly. "Yes, I suppose it is."

5

The egg hadn't hatched by the time they put down at a remote port near their base camp. Just as well—Aran wasn't sure he'd be able to smuggle a hatched land-devil inside his coat pocket like he had the egg (lined, of course, with all the protective linings they'd brought with them, and already beginning to smoke).

"You're a hundred percent sure this is going to be safe." Istvay's voice was as flat as their expression as they stepped down from the rickety transport the two of them had taken from the port to where they'd have to hike in to camp, and into the warm, pine-scented air of the northern Rim Mountains.

Aran nodded, trying very hard to keep his mind focused on Istvay's words instead of the tiny, helpless egg in his pocket. "I checked. I did an analysis on the acid from the egg, and assuming it's a similar composition to the acid they spit, the materials from the kennel shouldn't melt. It'll be perfectly safe. We can keep her there until she's well-trained enough that—"

"Aran!" Istvay's voice was incredulous. "This is a land-devil you're talking about! That's not a pet, it's an assassination attempt!"

From Aran's pocket came another small, muffled chirrup.

Istvay swore. "Well, we'd better get up to camp before the damn thing hatches. I guess that's our only option right now, short of just setting it loose on an unsuspecting planet."

"They're actually very fragile as infants. It's going to need constant care—"

Istvay had already started down the dirt trail that wound through the thick evergreen forest, irritation clear in the set of their shoulders.

Aran sighed, and started after them.

When they reached the camp, Aran slipped on a pair of protective gloves and very gently deposited the egg inside the kennel. He closed the door, pulled off his gloves, and positioned a small portable heater on the corner next to the egg. He'd examined the data they'd gathered, and it seemed the ideal heat for land-devil eggs was just a few degrees warmer than human body temperature—a stroke of luck, actually, since that was probably the only reason she hadn't hatched out already.

Then he settled in beside the kennel, watching the tiny egg, his breath coming quick in his chest.

Istvay crouched next to him a few minutes later with a heavy sigh. "You're sure you know what you're doing?" they asked quietly.

Aran turned to them, and some of the giddy, effervescent excitement bubbling through his veins must have shown in his expression, because Istvay gave a rueful grin, shaking their head.

"It should hatch any minute now, I think," Aran whispered, his voice soft with awe.

Now that the egg was at the proper temperature, it was only about five minutes before an egg tooth poked through the wrinkly, translucent shell. Fingers trembling with excitement, Aran replaced his protective gloves and reached inside the cage, helping the tiny creature to peel back the shell as he'd seen the adult land-devils do.

And then she was free—a little wet and slimy from the inside of the egg, her tiny body scrunched and wrinkled, her bulbous eyes blinking up at him in helpless innocence.

"Istvay," he said, in tones of absolute wonder. "Istvay, look at her."

Something bumped against Aran's shoulder, and he glanced up just long enough to see what it was.

Istvay was holding out one of their leather waterskins, which looked about half-full. Aran gave his friend a questioning look.

"The parents fed them as soon as they were hatched," Istvay grumbled. "And since we don't have any half-digested animals around here, I thought a meat slurry like the one we used to attract the prairie snouts last year might do the trick. This should have a pretty similar nutrient profile, I think."

Aran stared at Istvay for a moment, something catching in his throat. "Pishti …" he began, looking down at the waterskin, then back up at his friend. "Pishti, I—"

Istvay shook their head with that crooked half-smile they had. "Better go ahead and feed her. She looks hungry."

Aran swallowed, and turned back to his new baby.

She was trying, awkwardly, to wriggle towards him, her bulbous eyes fixed on his face, her tiny, slender tentacles almost disproportionately small compared to her lumpy body. She was making small, questioning, hungry noises, and Aran pushed the waterskin inside the crate towards her.

She touched it inquisitively with the tip of a tentacle.

"It's food, sweetheart," he cooed. "It's good for you. Want to give it a try?"

She touched it again, and then she must have caught a whiff of the contents, or else her instincts finally kicked in. She pounced on it with a surprisingly violent motion and punctured it with her little beak, lapping the liquid up with contented purring as the contents of the skin spattered the floor of the kennel around her.

Aran watched, his entire chest warm, his heart a melted puddle of pure adoration.

"Isn't she the most beautiful thing you've ever seen in your life?" he murmured to Istvay in a dreamy tone. "Just look at her."

At last, the tiny creature finished her meal, and she looked up at him, innocence and trust in her bulbous eyes. She pulled herself closer to his hand, her movements adorably awkward, and nestled against his glove, purring softly.

"What should we call her?" Aran whispered, keeping his voice low to avoid disturbing the tiny creature.

He'd never seen anything more perfect in his entire life.

"What about, 'the reason the two of us will spend the rest of our lives in jail'?" Istvay muttered. "Or wait, I know, Total Annihilation."

Aran was too deliriously happy to be offended.

The hatchling wriggled closer, tightening her tiny tentacles around his finger.

He felt something sharp pierce through the thick fabric, and a pain more intense than anything he'd felt in a very long time shot up his arm like a lightning strike.

He swore. "Pishti. She's gonna need feeding every few hours, and some fresh water, and—" His words were slurring, his tongue refusing to obey him.

And then the entire world went black.

When Aran regained consciousness, he blinked his eyes open and looked around in confusion. Everything hurt, and his brain felt thick and slow, and it took him a few moments to remember where he was.

Their base camp. The northern Rim Mountains.

Then he tried to sit up quickly, and only managed to almost topple over, his sluggish muscles not nearly quick enough to keep up with his suddenly panicked brain.

"Aran? Aran!" Someone caught him by the shoulder, steadying him, and he turned to see Istvay. Their face was pale and haggard, and their voice cracked with exhaustion. "Aran, for hell's sake lie down! You just about died. You've been in a coma for forty-eight damn hours, and you scared the living hell out of me. Are you—"

"Ani!" Aran mumbled in panic.

Istvay frowned. "Aran? No, no, I'm Istvay. Who's—are you delirious? Let me check your temperature, maybe you should—"

"Ani!" repeated Aran impatiently. "Our baby. I think she looks like an Ani. Is she—is she—"

Istvay let out a long sigh, slumping back on their heels. "She's fine," they said flatly. "I've been giving her fresh food and water through the cage every day, and she's been eating well. And I replaced the heater, since she spat acid through the bars yesterday and melted the first one, and I've been keeping it at the temperature we measured from the land-devil nest. She seems healthy enough, but she's mostly just been curled up by the heater sleeping when she's not eating."

Aran blew out a sigh of relief and tried to sit up again, a little more slowly this time.

"How are you feeling?" asked Istvay.

For the first time, Aran noticed, with a stab of guilt, the thick worry in their tone.

"Um. Pishti," he said awkwardly. "I'm—I'm sorry. I'm fine, honest, it was just—I mean, she's a baby, so her poison isn't as strong as in the adults, and I was pretty sure about that, anyways, before I let her cuddle with my glove, so it was just—"

"So it just put you in a coma for forty-eight hours, instead of actually killing you outright," Istvay grumbled. "I've been injecting every damn antivenin we have in our supplies into you for the last two days, hoping you'd pull through. It was touch and go for a bit there."

The guilt in Aran's stomach twisted harder. "I'm—I'm sorry," he muttered, sitting up. "I'm really sorry."

Istvay shook their head ruefully. "I should be used to it by now, I guess. And, in fairness, you did it for me three months ago when we ran into that nest of spitting vipers." They sighed, and pushed themself to their feet. "I'll get you something to eat, you stay there."

After some trial and error, Aran discovered he could stand, with support. He was still a bit wobbly, but he was perfectly capable of walking, as long as he didn't try to move too quickly. He gathered up the antivenins and his bedroll and, with some effort, dragged them across the small clearing.

Istvay had spent the last forty-eight hours trying to save his life, he figured the least he could do was try to make their life a little easier.

He was finished by the time Istvay came back with food. He gulped if down gratefully, hardly tasting it, then pushed himself carefully to his feet again.

"Where are you going?" said Istvay, a sharp note of alarm in their tone.

"I'm going to check on Ani," Aran said over his shoulder. He tried to hide the happiness in his voice, but he wasn't sure he was entirely successful.

He made it over to the cage, barely, and then crouched, holding onto the edge of it for support. He took a couple of protective liners, slipping them over his hands, and then pulled on another set of gloves, the elbow-length ones this time.

"Aran! You're not going to—" Istvay began, alarm in their tone.

"Don't worry," he said. "We know now that the poison isn't going to kill me, even if she does prick me through the glove and the linings. And while you were getting the food, I put together everything just in case—I've got all the antivenins lined up, and I laid out my bedroll here by the cage, so you don't have to lug me anywhere. And I made up her food for the next three days, so you don't have to worry about it."

Istvay's expression was strained. "Aran. That's not what I'm—"

Aran was barely listening. He reached into the cage, a small, blissful smile forming on his face. "Ani," he cooed. "Hello there, sweetheart. Do you like your new name? Pishti thought of it—well, they said Total Annihilation, but we can call you Ani, right?"

The tiny land-devil perked up at his voice, her entire body turning an inquisitive yellow. She sidled diffidently over towards the gloves and then cuddled herself against them. He stroked her tiny, lumpy body, and her protuberant eyes closed to slits of contentment, her colour changing gradually to a deep, contented green.

"Hey, sweetheart," he whispered, as she purred against his glove. He could hardly speak for the thick knot in his throat.

He wasn't sure he'd ever been so happy in his life.

She gave a sleepy chirrup, and he felt a smile spread across his face like warm butter over toast.

Istvay crouched down beside him, and Ani bridled a little, giving them a suspicious growl.

"So much for gratitude," Istvay grumbled. "I've been feeding her the whole time you were passed out, and that's all she does for me. But look at her with you."

As if in response, Ani snuggled her body closer against Aran's gloves, her tiny tentacles twining around his finger. Her whole body was barely the length of his hand, and Aran had never been so smitten in his life.

"Oh, you beautiful, beautiful girl," he crooned.

A tentacle spike punctured the glove, and the two layers of protective lining. A familiar jolt of pain shot up Aran's arm, and as the blackness crowded in around his vision, he turned to Istvay happily. "I think she likes me," he murmured.

And then he passed out.

It had been … well, Aran wasn't exactly sure how long it had been, all things considered. He'd lost track of time somewhere in the blur of caring for Ani, and getting knocked senseless, and then waking up and checking on Ani.

Istvay, he noticed guiltily, was looking distinctly haggard. But Ani was thriving. And Aran had learned several interesting things— although tentacle spikes could knock him out for up to seventy-two hours at a stretch, the more times he got stung, the less effective they became. Now he was at a point where he might only black out for fifteen minutes or so. The bites were similar, but the venom in Ani's bites must be a different type than in her tentacle spikes, because it gave him completely different symptoms. Other than knocking him unconscious, of course, both venoms did that. He had already planned some analysis of the substances, as soon as he could remain conscious for long enough to carry them out. The acid spitting was another matter. He had a few burns, and had melted through more protective suits than they probably could really afford. But he'd also learned, more or less, the kinds of things that made Ani want to spit.

She was growing in leaps and bounds. Every time he was awake, he'd make his way over to the cage and let her cuddle with his gloved hands, until she knocked him unconscious again.

He was crouched in front of the cage now, and Ani was purring contentedly, cuddled against his arm.

Istvay crouched beside him, looking like they hadn't slept in at least a week. Aran had commented on this, but Istvay had only growled that Aran looked a hell of a lot worse.

Which—was probably a fair point, all things considered. Still, he couldn't help the small pinch of worry in his chest.

"Aran." Istvay's voice was exhausted. "I don't think this is a good idea."

Aran was about to protest. But when he looked at his friend, he couldn't bring himself to.

He'd tried to set things up to make it as easy as possible on Istvay, and had told them, time and again, they didn't actually need to sit up with him when he was unconscious, he'd be completely fine. But they seemed to have decided to pay no attention whatsoever.

And something about the way the exhaustion drew dark circles under their eyes, and hollowed out their cheeks just a little, made Aran's stomach clench in concern.

Istvay sighed. "Aran. Listen. How about this? I promise that I'll get tested next time we're in do Sol like you keep harassing me to, as long as you promise to stop bloody trying to get your murder-pet to poison you. Okay?"

"Okay," he said. His voice was a little hoarse, probably an aftereffect of either the poison or the antivenins, but he was pretty sure it would get better soon. "Okay, Pishti. I won't get her to sting me just to test. Let me just finish feeding her, and then we can—"

Behind him, one of the camp stools, which had been partway knocked over when Aran stood, toppled.

Ani made a startled noise, and before he could pull away, Aran felt the now-familiar jab of a tentacle spike.

Istvay jumped reflexively to catch him, but he sucked in a deep breath and blinked hard against the pain shooting up his shoulder, concentrating on keeping the black that was crowding the edges of his vision from overtaking it completely.

And then, slowly, the blackness retreated.

He grinned at Istvay, a little shakily. "Look, Pishti! It doesn't even —it doesn't even knock me out now. I think—" He had to stop quickly, clamping his mouth shut against the sudden wave of nausea.

Istvay gave a long-suffering sigh. "Yes. I'm glad you didn't actually pass out this time," they said through their teeth. "Now, can you put her away, and maybe we can actually sit down and have a meal together for the first time since you started routinely poisoning yourself?"

The thought of food made the swell of nausea stronger, but Aran managed a nod anyways.

Istvay looked—well, more worried than he'd seen in a long time. He hadn't been paying that much attention, too focused on making sure Ani would survive in her new habitat, but—

He sighed, and pushed himself to his feet. Istvay caught his shoulder as he swayed.

"I'm—sorry, Pishti," he mumbled. "I just—"

Istvay sighed again. "I know," they said, resignation in their voice. "You just wanted to make sure your murderous tentacle-monster was safe and comfortable. I know you, Aran. I've known you since we were both five. Absolutely nothing about this situation surprises me."

Aran gave them a weak grin, and followed them on legs that were only slightly unsteady over to the campfire.

He couldn't actually eat much, but the hot coffee Istvay had brewed earlier that morning was surprisingly satisfying.

When the meal was done, Istvay leaned against the back of the camp stool and sighed. "So. Now that you can handle Ani without immediately passing out, I guess it's on to the next problem—how we're going to explain this to the rest of the planet. We still haven't made our final report to the counsellor who gave us permission to go."

Aran grimaced. "Um. About that. You know, we were planning on doing that expedition out into the far reaches of the southern Rim Mountains—"

Istvay rolled their eyes. "We can't just hare off to the ends of the earth, change our names and IDs, and avoid going back to Vila Nova do Sol ever again. You know that as well as I do. We have to get funding for our research somehow, and you know it'd kill you to keep everything we find to ourselves and never let the rest of the scientific community see it."

Aran gave a reluctant sigh. "Yeah," he muttered. "I—guess you're right."

"Look," said Istvay. "I've been thinking about this, while you were … well. Anyways. You were just awarded the Council's Medal for Scientific Advancement. You're probably the most famous scientist on the planet at the moment. If—" they held up a warning hand. "*If* you think you can get Ani trained well enough that she can at least pretend to be domesticated—" they shook their head. "I can't believe I'm saying this. I cannot honestly believe that I'm encouraging this. But, if you were to get her well-trained—look, all I'm saying is, if they'd trust anyone in the system with a land-devil for a pet—"

Aran glanced up, sudden hope rising in his chest. "You—you think they might—" he started.

Istvay sighed heavily. "I'm not saying it's a sure thing. But … like I said. If anyone would be able to talk the Council into it, it would be the scientist who recently got awarded the Medal for Scientific Advancement. You have a reputation when it comes to handling dangerous animals. I'm saying it's worth a try."

Aran glanced involuntarily over at the cage, where Ani was pressed up against the bars, watching them curiously. "And if—" he swallowed hard. "If they said no?"

Istvay gave a rueful shake of their head. "If they said no, I know someone I could talk into forging us new passports, and we'd head off into the southern Rim Mountains. I promise."

Aran stared at his friend for a moment, the warmth of gratitude in his chest almost too much to breathe through.

"Pishti," he began, then broke off, unable to find the words.

Istvay grinned at him reluctantly. "You think I'd let you go have all the fun by yourself?" They glanced back over the cage, and Aran could see the way their face softened, just a little. "Besides," they grumbled. "I—okay, I can't believe I'm saying this, but—well, but that thing is kinda cute."

They turned back to the campfire, squeezing their hand to activate their palmscreen, their face suddenly businesslike. "Alright. So, if we're going to do this ... While you've been—otherwise occupied, we got an invitation to a scientific gathering in do Sol in about a month's time. That might be the perfect opportunity to feel things out, figure out the best way to bring this up."

Aran had to bite back a curse.

He hated scientific gatherings. In fact, given the option, he'd much rather be rendered unconscious by land-devil venom than attend a scientific gathering. He'd hated them since he was a university student, and they'd only gotten worse with his newfound celebrity status—it seemed everywhere he went reporters wanted to ask him questions, old classmates who he distantly remembered as faces brushing past him in the hallway without sparing him a second glance were suddenly eager to claim friendship, and there was a bewildering amount of subtext and jostling for positions that he couldn't understand and quite frankly didn't want to.

"I know, Aran," said Istvay, their voice sympathetic. "But … you're currently the owner of the most deadly creature in the system, so …"

Aran took a deep breath.

For Ani, he could do this.

"That—sounds like a good idea," he said, the words almost choking him. "Let's tell them we'll be there."

6

Aran and Istvay got off the transport and settled themselves into the seedy hotel on the poor end of town without incident, mostly because Ani was still small enough to fit in the pocket of Aran's jacket, and he'd managed to soothe her with small pieces of raw meat so that she forgot her natural curiosity in her greedy delight.

"Damn that bloody bastard to hell," Istvay growled irritably from where they were sprawled out in one of the questionable-looking armchairs in the corner of the room.

Aran looked up from the feeding Ani another small chunk of bloody meat as she wandered curiously around the battered tabletop. "What's wrong?"

Istvay scowled at him. "Emeric is going to be there. I should have known. He's probably getting ready to delight in his status as most well-known member of our graduating class, now that he thinks he managed to knock you off."

Aran sighed. Still, he wasn't going to argue with Istvay, not after the month both of them had had. "I doubt he'll want to talk to either of us, honestly," he said instead. "And if he was trying to kill us, his plan didn't exactly work. So—"

Istvay shut down their palm screen, grumbling to themself about why did they even try, and Aran watched them fondly, until Ani nipped his finger with her sharp beak, jolting him back to his duties as provider of snacks.

He grinned at her as he held out another chunk of raw meat. Now that Ani was letting them both get some actual sleep and the dark, worrying circles under Istvay's eyes had finally disappeared, Istvay's familiar irritability was as soothing and comforting as a cup of hot coffee in the morning.

By the time the transport dropped them off outside the imposing government building, Aran's earlier discomfort had turned into a dull panic. He could hardly force his leaden legs to step out of the transport.

Istvay, bless them, paid the driver, then took Aran's elbow. "I accepted the invitation in my name," they said into his ear. "They'll figure out you're here soon enough, but I thought this way at least we'd be able to get inside without being swarmed by reporters."

Aran gave his friend a look of wordless gratitude. They grinned back at him and winked, and Aran refused to think about the way it made his heart stutter. And then the two of them ducked into the building.

The grand reception room was dimly lit, classical music playing softly from a musicians troupe in one corner, broadcast into the centre of the room via holoprojection. The guests mingled easily, the soft hum of conversation and clink of glasses making a counterpoint to the music.

There were enough people here that Aran could feel the waves of panic-induced nausea rising in his stomach, and he had to swallow hard to hold them back as he worked his way to the back of the room. If he stayed out of the way, he might not be noticed, at least for a while.

"I'll bring us back some drinks," Istvay whispered. They were grinning that mischievous grin of theirs, the one it was almost impossible for Aran to look away from.

Aran gulped, and nodded.

Istvay hesitated a moment. "Um. And we're not going to accidentally murder all the guests, are we?"

Aran opened the front of his suit jacket, peering down at where Ani was tucked into his inner pocket.

She pulled herself up with the tip of a tentacle, peeking one bulbous eye out, and he smiled despite himself.

He wasn't necessarily planning on introducing her at the gathering. But all things considered, he and Istvay had decided that she'd be safer here, supervised, than at the hotel room, unsupervised. There was always the possibility of an unwary hotel staff opening the door, and even if they didn't, Ani still tended to spit acid when she got upset. He wasn't sure having her melt a hole in the floor of the hotel room would do them any good on the public relations front.

Istvay shook their head, but they were still grinning reluctantly as they started off. Aran watched them navigate the crowded area around the refreshments table, their worn suit standing out among the expensive outfits of the rest of the company.

It wasn't that he and Istvay couldn't afford suits if they really needed them. It just—well, it seemed silly, considering they could use the money for their expeditions instead. And besides, the two of them were in do Sol as infrequently as either of them could manage. They'd both grown up here, and Aran had a sneaking suspicion that Istvay had as many uncomfortable memories of the city as he did.

Istvay had almost reached the table, and Aran was watching them with a small, familiar ache in his chest, when someone stepped up, barring Istvay's way.

Aran tensed.

It was Emeric.

"Come on, Ani," he whispered, and moved a little closer to where his friend was standing.

He could tell by the stiffness in Istvay's posture that this interaction was not going to go well, and furthermore, that Istvay had no intention that it should.

"I suppose I should offer you my condolences," Emeric was saying in his smooth voice when Aran got close enough to overhear. "I'm so very sorry that Aran was … unable to make it." Emeric's expression was almost sincere, but there was a sparkling glint of malice in his eyes.

He'd always hated Istvay.

Istvay gave him a thin-lipped smile. "I appreciate your concern," they said, the acid in their tone so strong that it could have matched Ani's. "I'm sure you were hoping to see him. I hear most of the planet wants his autograph these days. He doesn't give it out much— he just doesn't have time, to be honest—but he might make a special exception for you if you asked him nicely. After all, it must be so useful when you're looking for funding for your research to say you graduated in the same class as Aran Romeu."

Emeric's expression turned so molten that Aran was almost surprised Istvay's jacket didn't spontaneously ignite from the heat of it.

"You're trying to keep his death under the radar, I assume," Emeric hissed. "You want to do your own research and use Aran's name to get it noticed, is that it? You think if you hide it long enough, no one will know? Well, I know. And I'll make sure I ruin you, Istvay. I'll have every damn reporter in the city after you, and every damn police officer investigating you for your part in the death of the famous Aran. I have connections, unlike some homeless, penniless orphans I know, who got into university on public charity. And if you don't spend the rest of your damn life in prison, I—"

Aran stepped forward, clearing his throat.

Emeric looked up, then started, his face going suddenly pale.

"Aran?" he asked after a moment. "What are you—"

He paused, visibly regaining control. "Aran! It's so good to see you. I was just telling Istvay here—"

Aran stepped closer. "Back the hell away from Istvay," he said bluntly. "I heard exactly what you were telling them."

Istvay was looking between Aran and Emeric, eyebrows raised.

Emeric's eyes narrowed. "I don't know what you're insinuating, Aran, but …"

"I'm not insinuating anything. Stay the hell away from my friend."

There was a moment where Emeric glanced between the two of them, as if unsure of his next move. Then he smiled, a small, unpleasant smile.

"Aran," he said, stepping closer, his voice hardly louder than a whisper. "I should have known you'd be too much of a coward to take advantage of the opportunity I sent you. But then, when you're scared of space travel, it's hard to get much done, isn't it?" His smile widened, just a little, and there was something ugly behind it. "You think you can threaten me? You think you're better than me? You? The Rim Mountain foster kid and his homeless best friend, you think you can stand here and tell me what I can and can't do?

"You think just because you're famous, you can get away with anything. And you know what? Maybe you're right. Maybe you're so high and mighty now that no one can touch you. But you know who isn't? Your friend here. Istvay. And I promise you, Aran—I will ruin them. I can do it, too, you know I can. I'll make their life hell. I'll throw every obstacle in their way that I can dig up, and believe me, I can dig up a few. And you'll have the option of abandoning them as a research assistant, or abandoning your damn scientific career. Maybe you're untouchable at the moment. But I'll make Istvay's name poison. And I'll start right now, when they attack me unprovoked, because they're not damn well civilized enough to be in polite company without starting a fight." He reached out, grabbing the collar of Istvay's jacket.

Istvay was still standing frozen, staring between Emeric and Aran.

Aran was too angry to think about what he did next.

He stepped forward, dipping his hand into the inner pocket of his suit jacket.

Ani gave an inquisitive chirrup, but climbed willingly onto his fingers.

"You're wrong, Emeric," he said, stepping between him and Istvay. "You're wrong that I didn't take the opportunity you sent me."

Emeric frowned at the sudden change in topic. "You—" he began.

Aran pulled his hand out from under his jacket. "Meet Ani."

The tiny eye-pouches under Ani's eyes puffed up, and she growled.

There was a moment where Emeric just stared, as if he wasn't quite sure he could believe what he was seeing.

Then his eyes bugged in horrified shock, his face going an unattractive grey. "Aran!" he gasped. "Aran, you—you didn't actually —"

Aran smiled, fury still pounding through his veins. "She's a baby right now. Her venom won't actually kill you. But she's growing. And land-devils are very smart, and extraordinarily protective. If someone was interfering with me, or with Istvay, in any way, ever again—she'd be perfectly capable of tracking them down and killing them, in a very unpleasant way."

"I—" The look on Emeric's face was pure terror.

"So I suggest you leave Istvay the hell alone. I suggest you leave me the hell alone. I suggest you not tamper with our gear, or hire people to come after us, or whatever the hell you thought might be a good idea. Because the only person right now who's keeping Ani from going on a rampage is me."

He smiled wider, and grabbed Emeric's wrist with the hand that still held Ani. Ani hissed at Emeric's unfamiliar scent and reached out a delicate tentacle.

Emeric just had time to make a strangled sound before his eyes rolled back in his head. Aran stepped back as he collapsed, letting him land hard.

Istvay was staring between Aran and the fallen Emeric, and there was the hint of absolute delight in their grin.

"Well," they said at last. "We were looking for a time-limit for telling the Council about Ani. How long do you guess he'll be out?"

Aran shrugged. "Three days, give or take?"

"Good," said Istvay, satisfaction in their voice. "I'll see if I can get us a meeting with the Council tomorrow. Now, come on, let's get some drinks and talk to everyone we need to talk to so we can get out of here. Someone will notice Emeric eventually."

Aran grinned back despite himself, tucking Ani back into his pocket. "Good girl," he whispered, as she twined around his fingers with a contented purr. "You're such a wonderful little girl, aren't you?"

"You know," said Istvay, scooping up two glasses of wine from the table and handing one to Aran, "you're beginning to convince me that she really is."

7

Epilogue

Next evening

Aran dropped back, exhausted, into the hotel's dingy armchair, pulling the hood of his jacket down over his eyes. Even with the shaky relief washing through him, every muscle in his body was tight, and he was fighting back the absolute, sickening panic still jittering through him that always came when he had to stand in front of a whole damn group of people, with the noise and flash of the cameras and the reporters and the shouted questions.

Ani gave a sweet little chirrup, clambering up his jacket onto his shoulder, and despite everything, he managed a small smile at her.

Istvay came over to perch on the arm of the chair, grinning broadly, and something about their grin made Aran's own smile a little more genuine.

"You did it, Aran! I honestly wasn't sure we'd be able to convince them, but you did it. You're bloody brilliant, you know that?" Their smile softened, and Aran's heart jumped, and he had to swallow hard, because there was something about those brown eyes staring into his, framed by those ridiculously long lashes …

He cleared his throat and turned to tickle Ani under the chin.

"You hear that, girl?" he whispered. "You get to stay with us. I mean, you would have anyways, because we weren't ever going to give you up, no matter what the Council said. But we don't have to worry about that now, because the Council saw what a good, sweet, clever girl you are, and they said you could stay." He rubbed her head gently, and her colour changed slowly to a deep, contented green that spread down her tentacles, her eyes closing to slits. "Don't worry, I'd never let anyone take you away, sweetheart. And nor would Pishti. They love you too, even if they are cranky about it."

Istvay snorted, and Aran glanced up at them, grinning.

"I told you you'd be good," Istvay said. "You're brilliant, Aran. I mean it."

"Just don't ever ask me to go in front of the Council ever again," Aran mumbled. "It's going to take me a bloody week to recover from that."

"Well," said Istvay, raising an eyebrow mischievously, "you were talking about that expedition to the southern Rim Mountains we had planned. I heard some of the councillors making noises about holding a dinner for us tomorrow night, but if we were to sneak off tomorrow morning before they could ..."

There was a soft *ding,* and Istvay glanced up, frowning, then looked down at their wavelink.

From the corner of his eye, Aran could see them stiffen. And something about the change in their posture, the tiny, almost imperceptible pinch of their lips, shot a bolt of icy dread through his stomach.

"Pishti?" he asked, turning quickly. "What ..."

And then his eyes caught on Istvay's palmscreen, and his mind made sense of the words.

Regret to inform you ... results of your test ... positive ... come in to discuss

...

For a moment, he couldn't breathe.

He couldn't think, he couldn't feel anything, because it wasn't possible. This couldn't be happening, it wasn't possible that Istvay had the defect.

It wasn't possible that Istvay was dying, and that there was nothing either of them could do about it.

Istvay was his entire world. And he couldn't imagine his entire world just ending like this.

Ani made a little, worried sound, her tiny tentacles tightening on his skin, and pressed herself against his neck, and the warmth of her did something, at least, to bring him back to himself.

He swallowed hard, and glanced over at Istvay.

Istvay sat where they were, staring straight ahead, lips pinched tight, every muscle in their body tense. And Aran could see it in them, see how they were bracing themself to turn and comfort *him*

...

He took a deep breath and pushed himself to his feet. "Pishti." He crouched in front of them, placing a hand on their shoulder like they'd done so often for him. "Pishti, listen to me. We're going to get through this. You haven't even started showing symptoms yet, that means we have a few years. We'll figure this out, okay?" His voice shook, just a little, but he managed to keep his words mostly steady.

Finally, Istvay looked up at him, and Aran had to fight back another wave of blind, unreasoning terror. Their face was set, but their expression was haunted, and he could see the fear in their eyes that they were trying to hide.

"Pishti," he began again, voice choking.

Somehow, they managed a smile. "Aran. It's ... fine. It's okay. I ... we both knew this was a possibility. And it's not like there's anything we can do about it, so—"

"No." Aran cut them off sharply. His heart was pounding sickeningly in his chest. "No. We're not giving up. You're not giving up. We're going to find something to fix this. Hell, we're damn scientists. If anyone can do something—"

Istvay shook their head, their expression fond and infinitely weary. "People have been searching for a cure for—what, five hundred years, give or take? I'm sorry, but ..." They shrugged helplessly. "Maybe it's best if we just—"

"Shut up, Pishti," he snapped. "We just got back from an expedition to look for land-devils, which was supposed to be unsurvivable. We brought back Ani. We talked the Council into letting us keep her. And I'm damn well not giving up on this before we even start. Okay?"

Istvay blinked at him in surprise. At last they smiled, the expression a little more genuine this time. "Okay," they said quietly. "Okay. We won't give up just yet."

Aran closed his eyes and sucked in a deep breath, feeling suddenly dizzy. "Yeah," he said.

"And ..." Istvay glanced around. "Either way, it's not like there's anything the doctors can do. So no point in staying here any longer than we have to." Their expression was still haunted, but their grin had regained a trace of its usual mischief. "If we're going to make our escape tomorrow morning so they can't rope us into a dinner, we should probably start getting our things together." They paused. "I mean, whatever things we have left that your damn land-devil pet hasn't melted," they grumbled.

Aran stared at them for a moment, and then he managed a small chuckle. "Yeah," he said. "Yeah, I guess we should."

Istvay slid off the arm of the chair, and for just a moment, they turned to him, their eyes meeting his. "Aran ..." they began in a quiet voice.

And then they turned away quickly, pulling down their battered knapsack and tossing it onto the bed.

Aran watched them, something tightening around his chest.

Ani gave a questioning little chirp, and he reached up absently to rub her head. "Don't worry, Ani," he whispered. "It'll be alright. It'll be fine. We'll figure this out."

He'd find a way to save Istvay. Whatever that meant, whatever it took, he'd do it.

And besides ... he glanced over at Ani, who was purring contentedly on his shoulder.

They'd just finished doing one impossible thing.

Now, somehow, they just had to find a way to make it two.

Book one of the Singularity, Redshift is available on Amazon

You might also enjoy The Ungovernable series, also by R.M. Olson.

A mouthy ex-smuggler pilot, a grumpy demolitions expert, a tech genius and a hacker. They're pulling a job on the most dangerous weapons dealer in the System. They're stealing tech that could change the course of history. And every one of them has something to hide.
What could possibly go wrong?
"Spectacular and thrilling! Olson's debut novel is filled with compelling characters and endless excitement." -SD Simper, author of the Fallen Gods series

You can order book one, Zero Day Threat, on Amazon.

I also have a Patreon, where I post character art, short stories, sneak peaks, and other fun stuff. You can get in on it for only $3/month, so if you're interested, check it out here!
https://www.patreon.com/rmolson

www.ingramcontent.com/pod-product-compliance
Lightning Source LLC
Chambersburg PA
CBHW021750190726
48290CB00008B/2555